About the Author

Morgan Wedlake was born in Barnstaple, England in 2003 and has always had an interest in literature and books. Currently studying Medieval History at university, Morgan enjoys the cinema, and is currently teaching himself the piano. *Chilling By The Waterfall* is Morgan's first published book.

Chilling By The Waterfall

Morgan Wedlake

Chilling By The Waterfall

Olympia Publishers
London

www.olympiapublishers.com
OLYMPIA PAPERBACK EDITION

A CIP catalogue record for this title is
available from the British Library.

ISBN: 978-1-80074-544-5

This is a work of fiction.
Names, characters, places and incidents originate from the writer's
imagination. Any resemblance to actual persons, living or dead, is
purely coincidental.

First Published in 2022

Olympia Publishers
Tallis House
2 Tallis Street
London
EC4Y 0AB

Printed in Great Britain

Dedication

For my family, who have supported me every step of the way.

Acknowledgements

I would like to first thank Olympia Publishers for giving me the opportunity to publish my first ever book. Special thanks to James Houghton, Kristina Smith, Sophie Grover and the whole team who helped my dream become a reality. I would also like to thank my family, especially my mum since, without her guidance, I would never have thought about publishing in the first place.

Introduction

As my first full story, *Chilling By The Waterfall* has been a long process. Perhaps longer than I thought it was going to take. Firstly, the plot was conceived in a swimming pool in Malta in 2017, with just me spit-balling a stupid idea with a friend, promising to write it before the summer ended.

Skipping to September 2017, the start of Year 10 for me, and with only a few chapters briefly written, I decided to forget about the story, leaving it to a memory of summer. Skipping two years and six months later, England was plunged into lockdown in March 2020, triggering me to dust off the family laptop and carry on with this ridiculous story. Over the next year and two months, I worked on it, on and off, sometimes taking days off and sometimes months.

However, on 10th May 2021, I finally typed the last word on the last page on the last chapter on the last sentence, freeing me of the promise I had made four years earlier in the smouldering heat of Malta. Was it worth it? Sure. It better have been. With this complete, I can concentrate on more complex and detailed stories that I have in mind, but this always will be the first, and for that, I will remember it forever.

Chapter 1

The Children

The cool, crisp wind that blew through the old town of Chillmont left a sharp pain on the four children's faces as they sat in a semi-circle chatting to each other, shaking but happy. The white blades of grass erecting from the ground were unaffected by the strong breeze. The tartan blanket the children sat on was buried deep in the frost and their chattering teeth echoed around the tall, naked trees that surrounded them. Facing the children's backs were seven large waterfalls that were stuck in mid-flow. The largest of the seven (which was directly in the middle) ended only a couple of metres behind the children. Its towering figure dwarfed the other six waterfalls and they were all at least three hundred metres in height. The four children varied in age but always travelled there every Saturday just to relax and celebrate the two days they had off school.

The tallest of the children was female and had long brown hair which slightly covered her sharp, dark eyes. Her pale body was covered in a large overcoat with thick trousers. The boy next to her was a few years younger and had broad shoulders and a large stocky body. His legs were stretched out, covering at least half of the blanket. Next to his tree-trunk legs were the opposite, small, thin legs connected to a slightly larger body with a beachball head and tight, ginger pigtails. Her forehead was slightly creased and her mouth was small with rabbit teeth protruding from her gums. To her left, was a boy of around seven years who had messy, black hair and was wearing a grey puffa jacket over his bony body.

"Hey, Ellie! Can you remember what happened this time last week?" said the brown-haired female to the ginger, stinging the air with her cloud of breath.

"Oh yeah, when Rodgerico slipped in the snow and banged his head on a rock!"

All of a sudden, the burley boy burst out laughing and banged the carpet with his vast hands which made the small boy clutch his ears.

"Why did you have to bring that up, Roxie?" Rodgerico screamed at the oldest girl of the group. His hand massaged the large bump that was still prominently sticking out of his scalp.

"Shut up, Rodg," Roxie said, "you made Ewan jump." The small boy jumped up, ran over behind Roxie and planted his small hands on her shoulders.

"I'm not a baby, Roxie!" he shouted in her ear and shook her quite hard.

"Get off!"

Ewan jogged back to his space and sat down making the snow crunch and blanket crease.

With everyone back in their original place, Roxie felt the cold breeze dig into her as she hugged her knees, the same position she was in when …

Chapter 2

The Murder

...her dad had come home drunk. Roxie was used to this on a weekly basis. Every Friday and Saturday, her dad came home, always stinking of alcohol and laughing, shouting or sometimes vomiting on the settee. He used to go down to the pub around seven and come back around eleven. His usual pub was 'The Golden Skunk' and his favourite drinks were pints of beer or cider. During the week, Roxie used to hear him bragging to his friends that he had 5 pints of alcohol every Friday night. When he came home, he almost always went to bed and his snores always kept Roxie awake till gone midnight. She always watched her favourite TV show every Friday and Saturday from a quarter to ten till a quarter to eleven.

This particular Friday night, Roxie was just getting ready for bed in her bedroom when she heard her father stomp in and slam the door behind him. She listened out for his friendly laughter or cheerful shouting but all she heard was his heavy boots stomping quickly towards the kitchen where her mother was clearing up. Confused, Roxie quickly slipped on her pyjamas and crept downstairs towards the kitchen. Her slippers made the stairs creak and her hands slid down the banister as if they were greased. As nervous as an eight-year-old would be in that situation, she reached the bottom of the stairs and turned right, shuffled forward, turned right again and crept towards the kitchen. Roxie stood in the open doorway and saw her parents shouting at each other. Her dad was standing there with an empty pint glass in his left hand while his right hand was clenched in a fist by his side. Her mum was jabbing her left forefinger in Roxie's dad's face. Roxie heard the occasional word she understood like 'Sam' (her father's name), 'Wendy' (her mother's name), 'baby' and 'never', but it was mostly just white noise to her.

Suddenly, out of nowhere, her father raised his shaking hands, smashed the glass over Wendy's head and curled his hands around her throat. Wendy's shaking hands felt along the table-top until she grasped a kitchen knife from the table beside her and plunged it deep into Sam's chest. He grasped the handle that was embedded in his chest. Almost gracefully, he slumped to the ground and lay still, blood pouring out of him like the water fountains Roxie had seen at school. Horrified, Roxie let out a piercing scream and Wendy turned around to face her. She looked between her screaming child and her dead husband. Roxie turned around and ran as fast as she could upstairs and into her baby brother, Rodgerico's, bedroom. Crying, she launched onto his bed and hid under the covers, soaking the mattress. From downstairs she heard her mother shouting her name as she walked upstairs, also crying. Roxie just laid there, crunched up on her brother's bed as the cold reality of her father's death hit her…

Chapter 3

The Snowball

…in the back of the head, showering her overcoat with white flakes and making it look like she had terrible dandruff. Roxie stood up, shaking from the cold water that crept down her back and the memory she had just relived a moment ago.

"GOTCHA! WHAT A SHOT!" Rodgerico shouted from across the frozen field. His gloved hands were also flaked with snow which didn't dampen the warm grin across his face. His fist pumped the air and he pointed and laughed at Roxie's white, spotted hair. Infuriated, Roxie ran towards Rodgerico and pushed him as hard as she could into the snow, creating a wave of it that coated the other children. He got up and immediately ducked as another snow missile narrowly missed him, fired by Roxie. Hiding behind a tree, Rodgerico started to sculpt a new snowball.

Only a few minutes later, he had created a small pyramid of ammo. Gleefully, Rodgerico piled five into his right hand and clenched one in his left. With his back hugging the bark, he dared a look around the tree, scoping out for an easy target. Out of nowhere, Rodgerico's…

Chapter 4

The Neighbour

…legs were caught under Roxie's weight as she flumped onto his bed. He woke with a start and propped himself up in his bed. He looked down at his crying sister, a million thoughts flying through his head. He heard his mum walking up the stairs, shouting his sister's name. Confused, Rodgerico got out of bed and went out onto the landing. He saw his mum, standing halfway up the stairs with what looked like ketchup all over her hands and sleeves. She was crying like Roxie, her head in her hands and shaking all over like she was in the Arctic.

"Are you okay, mummy?" Rodgerico asked, with a nervous whisper.

"NO, I AM NOT OKAY RODGERICO!" Wendy shrieked. "NOW CAN YOU GO BACK TO BED!"

The doorbell rang, which made Rodgerico jump a little. Shaking a little too, he walked past his weeping mother to answer the door. Standing in the doorway was Mr White. He was Rodgerico's neighbour and lived to the right. Rodgerico always saw Mr White walking his bloodhound every Tuesday morning when he was being driven to rugby practice. He always had a large smile, which his dog always matched, its tongue falling out of its open, panting mouth. He always gave a hearty wave and Rodgerico returned the favour every time they passed each other, usually with a mud-caked one which always made him chuckle.

But, standing in the doorway now, there was no large smile or hearty wave. His face was only the face of concern and worry and uneasiness.

"Is everything okay in here?" White asked in a deep voice. "I heard screaming."

"Well, my mum is crying on the stairs and I don't know why."

"Well, may I come in and try and sort it out?"

"All right."

Mr White strolled in and had a short, quiet conversation with his mum. Their voices were almost the polar opposite. His mum's was quick and frantic: Mr White's was slow and steady. After the conversation ended, Rodgerico's mum pointed a pale, shaking finger at the kitchen. Mr White brushed past the still weeping woman and marched into the kitchen. Almost automatically, Rodgerico followed him.

Rodgerico was speechless. He saw his dad, lying on the tiled floor, blood spilling out onto the floor. His dad's lifeless, dilated eyes were staring up at the ceiling. Mr White was also in a state of shock but he seemed to get over it more quickly than Rodgerico did. He immediately whipped out his iPhone and quickly dialled '999' into the pad. He put it to his ear and started talking very quickly. Rodgerico decided to walk away and stagger up the stairs (passing his mum again) to enter his sister's room. He also started to cry, his tears rolling...

Chapter 5

The Mother

…through the snow after being pelted by two ultra-large snowballs. Roxie was lying next to him and laughing, his ammo reduced to slush.

"Oh my God. You just got destroyed!"

As Roxie laughed and Rodgerico shook off the remaining flakes of snow, about a mile away down the road and in the third house on the left of Redwood Avenue was their mother, Wendy. She had just finished clearing up the dinner table. As she was wiping the table, she glanced up to look up at the large mirror that hung on the wall. Staring back at her was a 50-year-old, thin, pale woman who had sunken eyes and a garnet jumper loosely hanging from her body. She had black leggings on and ankle socks (which you couldn't see in the reflection). Wendy chucked the soaked cloth back into the sink, put the kettle on and walked into the living room. She sank into her favourite chair and felt the thick velvet which almost comforted her thoughts. As she leaned back into the armchair, she fell back into her thoughts and into the past but was disturbed because she…

Chapter 6

The Prison

…heard the sirens slowly advancing towards the house, knowing what was surely to follow. Her sweaty, bloody hands were playing with each other. She heard the sound of the door opening and people running into the kitchen and towards her.

Two policemen came into the room. One of them lifted her up and the other handcuffed her hands behind her back. The cold metal of the cuffs tightened on her thin wrists. They led Wendy away, shaking, one hand on each of her shoulders, escorting her out through the doorway and into the police car where they thrust her head down into the back seat. One of the policemen sat next to her, clutching her arm while the other got into the driver's seat and started the engine. Wendy glanced out of the tinted windows of the car and saw both her children standing in the doorway. They were pale, shaking, and their faces were streaked with tears. Ashamed, Wendy looked down at her lap and didn't look up for the rest of the journey.

After what felt like forever, they arrived at the Police Station. The policeman next to her opened the door and practically dragged her out into the fresh air. The other policeman also got out of the car and grabbed her other arm, making sure she had no chance of escape.

The lobby looked how people would probably feel if they

entered a Police Station: grey and dull. The chairs, walls, floors, and ceiling — even the secretaries' faces were grey. The policeman, who held Wendy's right shoulder, let her go and had a short chat with the receptionist. He came back with a small plastic bag while a female officer came and searched her. Her purse, keys and glasses were taken away from her and put into a plastic bag. Her shoelaces were also taken away as she was led to a tiny cell, which stunk of wee and blood. The policeman didn't even speak to her. He just slammed the door and walked away. She listened to his footsteps slowly fading away as she lay down on the mattress and felt her emotions wash over her. Fear, panic, relief, disgust, hate, pity, determination. Wendy lay back and thought about all of these until she slowly slipped out of consciousness and into a deep, uncomfortable sleep.

* * *

About 8 months later, Wendy was imprisoned in Chillmont Institution. The court case which had been carried out about a month earlier was a very sickening experience for her. The hardest part was seeing her children as witnesses, talking about that night and the instant regret as the judge condemned her to twenty-five years in Chillmont Institution. Just seeing her children's faces as she was escorted out of the court made her feel sick.

She now sat in a smaller cell than the one she had been held in on that night and it stank of more things than just wee and blood. She just sat there, thinking for a while and then laid down on the bed and prodded the mattress which leaned inches over her and was only held up with a couple rods of iron.

A rugged man's face of about forty with a 5 o'clock shadow

leaned over to stare at Wendy as she lay in her own, comfortable clothes. The time was five minutes to two (according to the low-hanging clock on the wall of their cell). This meant that it was only five minutes until the guards finished their two-hour lunch break and they came and unlocked the prisoners to get them back to work. Wendy and Alex (who was the man lying on the top bunk), however, had different ideas.

During these 5 minutes, Wendy went over the plan that they had been planning for weeks.

"Step 1: You knock out the guard as he comes to unlock us. Then, you wear his uniform and walk out without showing your face. You then let me go to work. You with me so far?"

With this, Alex nodded and Wendy continued.

"Step 2: You head to the safe and enter the four-digit code into the safe. Grab the key, close the safe and head to the washing room. I then fake my death and you take me to through to the main exit. You unlock the door and walk out towards the garage. You hot-wire the car and then we're away. Make sure you head to the cave. You remember… and stick it out there until we lose the police. Then, you drive to that abandoned building, we ditch the car and we stay there for a couple of days. We then get some money, somehow, and get some plastic surgery. We then get jobs, buy a house, get my kids back and live out our happy lives together."

Alex was nodding throughout Wendy's monologue and, right at the end, he started to shake and rub his hands. This made the bunk bed nearly topple over. The time was now one minute to two, which meant one minute until their plan was to be put into place.

"Right, get in position Alex. The rest of our lives begin now."

Chapter 7

The Breakout

At exactly 2 p.m., Officer Trusslley sauntered towards the cell which held Wendy and Alex. He spun the keys around on his finger as he got to the front of the barred door. He slipped the key into the lock, hearing it snap open. He clutched the bars and dragged it open to its fullest.

"Oh, my goodness, Officer! Thank goodness you're here," Wendy shrieked as she ran towards Trusslley.

"What seems to be the problem, miss?"

"It's my… um… my partner! He, uh, he…he just said he… um… um… he felt really sick and… um… he went to go and lie down and… uhhhh… he suddenly won't wake up and I'm really scared for him! Can you please help me?"

Sighing, he walked into the cell and saw Alex lying in his bed. The sheet was soaked with sweat and his brown hair was poking out from under the covers.

"Excuse me, sir. Are you okay?"

As quick as a flash, Alex leaped out of bed and pushed the officer against the wall of the cell. The loud sound rattled in Trusslley's ears as he felt a sharp pain slowly crawl up his back. Alex's hand clenched into a fist and made hard, sharp contact with the side of his head. He slumped down against the wall, unconscious. Excited that their plan was working, Wendy told Alex to pull the guard behind the bed quickly. Wendy quickly re-explained the plan as Alex changed into Trusslley's uniform. Wendy then quickly joined the large group of inmates heading to work and Alex lost sight of her in the large crowd of orange. Once the prisoners had departed, Alex left the cell and locked it up behind him. Thinking about Wendy's plan, he headed towards the safe. He passed a couple of guards but kept his head down and shoved his hands into his pockets.

After two near misses and several wrong turns, Alex finally made his way towards the safe. It was quite hidden and out of place, just jutting out of the wall like a blackhead on a celebrity. As Alex walked up to it, he brought out Trusslley's ID card. It had all his information on it but, also, scrawled on the bottom, were four digits.

Wendy had carefully planned this escape and wanted everything to be perfect. So, she had remembered that the guard who usually unlocked them after lunch was very forgetful. She had made sure that Alex took this officer's uniform because she had known that he would forget the four-digit code for the safe and, therefore, would have written it down somewhere.

Happy that Wendy was much cleverer than him, Alex punched in the code and opened the thick, metal door. In the safe lay a large key with a thickness similar to the safe it was held in. Alex grabbed the key and it felt cold in his hand. It was as if it knew that he was doing something wrong. He pushed it deep into his pocket and headed towards the washroom.

After fifteen minutes and a few close calls from the other guards, Alex opened the door to the washroom. The sound of the washing machines whirring filled his ears and his eyes swivelled, just like the machines. He spotted Wendy down at the very end of the room, just sitting on the bench watching the clothes roll over each other in the machine. Alex walked past the other working prisoners and sneaked up behind her. He tapped her on the shoulder and nodded to her, secretly. This was the signal to continue with the plan. As Alex hung back, Wendy clutched her chest and gasped for breath. She started shaking and fell onto all fours. Her hands grasped at nothing as her fingernails scraped the floor. She fell onto her belly then rolled onto her back, still gasping for breath. She then took one last deep breath, and her head smacked onto the floor as she lay still.

Alex raced over to Wendy and knelt down beside her and checked her pulse. His rough fingers moved over to her soft wrist and felt a strong pulse race into him.

"Nice acting."

"Thanks," Wendy whispered, barely moving her lips and keeping her eyes firmly shut.

"ALL RIGHT. EVERYONE STAND BACK!" Alex shouted, stretching his hands out to create space. "THIS INMATE HAS UNFORTUNATELY HAD A HEART ATTACK AND DIED! PLEASE STAY AWAY AND DO NOT PANIC! I WILL DEAL WITH THIS!"

A nervous chatter filled the washroom as he scooped Wendy up from the floor. Her arms swung underneath her and the prisoners moved out in a way similar to Moses parting the Red Sea. He walked out of the door and started towards the exit. His feet moved quickly and his palms started to get sweaty after gripping tightly to Wendy's body. Almost told by the gods, they didn't meet any guards on their journey to the exit. The large doors stood in front of the two criminals as they turned the last corner. Alex walked towards it and carefully put Wendy down, still to make the façade that she was dead stay true.

He pulled out the long key from his pocket and slotted it into the large hole placed carefully in the far right of the door. It easily twisted and pushed open as if it was made of nothing. Both Alex and Wendy were stunned that the plan was working this well.

Suddenly, they heard a shout from behind. A guard, the literal size of a gorilla and almost as hairy as one, was heading towards them down the corridor. His large thighs bulged under his uniform. His large fists scraped the floor as he lumbered towards them, screaming at the top of his lungs. Alex grabbed Wendy's hands and legged it outside. After they got out, both of them leaned on the door and pushed as hard as they could until the door clicked closed. They walked backwards away from the door. They could feel the floor vibrating with the guard banging on the door. Unfazed by this little hiccup, Wendy reminded Alex of the direction to the garage.

A guard was waiting outside the garage, his Glock-17 pistol strapped to his waist. Alex peered round the corner of the building and rested his head on the wall. "How are we going to reach the car now?" he thought. Wendy, however, was already thinking of another plan inside their original plan to get to the garage.

"Alex, listen. Since you still have the guard's uniform on, you can get close to him, right?"

"Correct."

"So — go on then!" Wendy hissed.

Alex tipped his cap and headed towards the armed guard. Quick as a flash, Alex pulled the handgun out of its holster and smashed the guard in the temple with the butt of the pistol. Knocked clean out, he slumped against the garage door. Wendy appeared round the corner and pulled the unconscious man out of the way of the door as Alex tried the handle.

"Wendy, it's locked!" Alex spat as he desperately turned the handle.

"Just shoot the lock then, you idiot!"

"Isn't that gonna attract a lot of people, though? Like the entire police force?"

"Well, you better be quick then."

Chapter 8

The Chase

Alex pointed the Glock-17 at the handle and hovered his finger over the trigger. His eyes were squinted and his breaths were slow. With shaking hands, Alex pulled the trigger and a deafening bang echoed around the Police Station walls. Looking around like a frightened cat, Alex slotted the gun into his pocket. Wendy grabbed the damaged handle and pulled it up revealing the five police cars that glinted in the bright sun.

"Come on!" Wendy shouted, and the pair raced towards one of the cars closest to the door. Using the butt of the gun again, Alex smashed the windows and the two of them clambered into the vehicle.

Meanwhile, multiple policemen were racing to the garage, armed with shotguns and assault rifles. Their hard boots slammed onto the concrete floor and their steady hands gripped tightly onto their loaded firearms.

Alex had successfully hot-wired the car and started the engine. The car roared like a lion that had just woken from its slumber. Alex's knuckles where white and bulging as they launched out of the garage like a bullet. The car swerved left and right as it aimed for the exit which was almost within reach. As the car turned the last corner, a row of policemen, were aiming their guns at the stolen car like a firing squad. Alex pushed his foot down harder onto the acceleration pedal and the car sped towards the line of guards.

The front window was the first sign that the guns had been fired. The glass collapsed inwards showering the two. Wendy and Alex ducked their heads so that their backs were parallel with the dashboard. Multiple bullets ricocheted off of the front and side of the car as Alex desperately tried to manoeuvre without even risking a glance at where they were going. Knowing that there was no way to exit via the proper exit, Alex desperately swung the wheel to the right and the car smashed through the gates. The alarms whined as bullets continued to implode at the rear of the motor. Dirt spurted up behind the wheels as the car made its way onto the road.

Alex's head peaked over the dashboard and he saw that there were no gun barrels pointing at him, so he decided that it was safe.

"We made it. I don't know how but we actually made it!"

Wendy also sat up straight in her seat and started laughing loudly.

"I can't believe that actually happened. We just broke out! We did it!"

"Now, all we have do is get to the abandoned house and we are done!"

Suddenly, the left-back wheel buckled and the car dramatically slowed. Alex's head whipped round and saw three police cars racing towards them. Hanging out of the backseat of each car were policemen with MP5SFA3s aimed straight at them. One of them had obviously just shot out the back wheel. And, they were gaining quickly.

"Give me the gun!" Wendy screamed. Alex, without looking down, whipped the pistol out of his pocket and dropped it into Wendy's lap. She picked it up and felt the shape of the gun in her hands. Her fingers played over the trigger, barrel and frame. She poked her head out of the window and aimed the gun at the car furthest to her left. Two shots fired in quick succession broke a headlight and the front window. However, being distracted by the left car, the right car crept up and drove level with Alex's window.

"Wendy! Quick!" Alex exclaimed. Wendy raised the gun and pulled the trigger. The bullet flew inches past Alex's nose and hit the policemen in the middle of the forehead. The man's head flew straight back and the car screeched to a halt. Petrol leaked out of the back, creating a rainbow puddle on the floor. Thinking fast, Wendy turned a 180 and pointed the gun at the growing petrol puddle. Just as the two police cars passed the wrecked one, Wendy shot the liquid.

A ball of orange, yellow and red expanded covering the entire road. A terrific heat hit Wendy like a fist. The car lurched forward and the two police cars flipped 20 metres into the air and landed with a screeching noise that rattled their ears. The pair spluttered on and Wendy sat back in her chair, still hearing the sound...

Chapter 9

The Fight

…of the kettle boiling. The high-pitched squeal disrupted Wendy from continuing with her short break. She groaned quietly as she pushed herself up from the armchair staggering a little as she stood. A small headache began erupting from the back of her head so she stumbled towards the medicine cabinet. She grasped the small knob and opened the mirrored door to reveal the multi-coloured pills and liquids scattered among the shelves. Wendy grasped at a random bottle and popped two pills into her mouth. Wendy headed back to the kitchen, pouring a glass of water and downing the entire glass, swallowing the pills in doing so. Shaking, she staggered towards the door, and left.

Back at the park, the four children had started a full-grown snowball battle: Ewan and Ellie versus Rodgerico and Roxie. The ground had become saturated with broken snowballs and four different sized footprints. Ellie got thrown to the ground by an unseen snowball to the back of the head and Ewan tripped over her flailing body. As Ellie laid there, water trickling into her jeans, she suddenly got…

Chapter 10

The Missing Father

...back from school. It was the first time Ellie had walked home by herself. She burst into the kitchen with a wide grin on her face and flew into the arms of her ecstatic mother. Her older brother and sister were smiling also, each either side of her mum. Wendy and Ellie held the embrace for some time until Wendy released her daughter and ruffled her hair playfully.

"Your dad would've been so proud of you!" Wendy said as she extended back to full height. Ellie thought back to the day her dad left and felt a tear brim in her eye (which she quickly wiped away, out of fear of mocking from her siblings).

It was just an ordinary day. The sun was shining and the birds were singing. The warm wind whipped throughout the house as Ellie sat in the front room watching TV. The windows were open and the bright light shone directly on to the screen making it difficult for Ellie to see the dancing cartoons. She heard the front door slam and she knew that her father was home. She heard his footsteps as they moved from the porch through the landing and into the kitchen. She heard him start a conversation with her mother and the voices became louder and louder.

Ellie was used to this. Nearly every day she and her siblings heard the shouts and shrieks of their parents but it happened so often that they had just become used to it.

But this day was different. The voices didn't quieten down

after a couple of minutes. Ellie's father, Alex, didn't come and see each of his children and ask them how their day was and tell them funny stories about his work and then go back to the kitchen to help Wendy, Ellie's mother, with dinner.

The voices didn't die down. They stopped abruptly and there was an awkward, uncomfortable silence. The sound of Alex's footsteps were harder, as he moved out of the kitchen, into the porch, and out of the house. No "hello." No questions. No funny stories. No dinner help. Nothing.

Ellie hoped every day that she would hear those footsteps come into the porch and come towards her. She hoped that he would bound in and tell her amazing stories about his life. But he had never returned since that day.

The tear crept down her cheek and dropped onto the tiled floor. Ellie's mum wiped her cheek, told her not to worry and that they were all proud of her. Feeling slightly better, Ellie…

Chapter 11

The Trip

...got hit in the face with another snowball. The sharp, cold pain spread over her face as she twisted onto her back and clutched her face. Ewan chuckled as he brushed his hands together to get rid of the remaining flecks of snow that originated from the snowball that he had just launched into his sister's face.

Around 150 metres in front of the waterfalls the ground began to deepen into a long steep hill which stretched well over 200 metres. It was this hill that Ewan forgot about as he ran, still giggling, away from his sister, expecting a counter-attack. A clump of snow sat on the top of the hill. Ewan's small feet and legs heavily collided with it and it sent him sprawling down the steep slope. He rolled and rolled...

Chapter 12

The Snowman

…the ball around the front garden until it grew taller than him. Ewan struggled to push the white sphere towards his sister who was standing a couple of metres away holding a ball about half of the size of the one which Ewan was moving. The thrill of creating a snowman for the first time sent exciting chills down his spine as he sprinted inside to fetch the facial features for the new life he was creating, outside.

"Enjoying yourself out there, son?" said Wendy as Ewan grabbed a carrot from the fridge, some coal from the fireplace and went back outside before he had time to answer.

The snow had fallen heavily the night before. All throughout the night the light flakes pattered on Ewan's window, keeping him wide awake with excitement. As soon as dawn broke, Ewan threw open his curtains and looked at the white blanket that covered everything from his front door to the curve of the road. Ewan wanted to go out immediately but his mother instructed him not to because he had work to do around the house. The day dragged until around three, consisting of cleaning the dishes and finishing his homework. Finally, Ewan was allowed out of the house and into his cool back garden. He smelt the air and the snow crunched under his small boots. The thrill of the sharp wind and the light flakes that still fell made Ewan shudder with glee. He started with the smallest one of the three, piling the fresh snow into his gloved, cupped, hands, slowly caressing and fondling it until it became a perfect sphere. Ewan then decided to tackle the largest of the three balls, beginning to create a ball similar to the one he had just created but placing it back onto the floor and rolling it around the ground. His sister came out and offered to help. He accepted gratefully because he was now struggling to push it.

And now, with Ellie's help, the snowman was complete. Its three-tiered body towered over Ewan and its arms were as long as Ewan's legs were. The jet-black eyes stared into the distance and its fixed smile drew up to where its ears ought to be. Its nose stuck out like Pinocchio. The force with which Ewan pushed it in had created little cracks that...

Chapter 13

The Cracks

…spider webbed across the top of the large waterfall, causing the children to jump. The cracks snaked their way down the fall, interlinking as they travelled all the way down. Roxie looked up and saw a figure, covered in shadow, striking the base of the waterfall with a mallet, three, four, five times before it disappeared like a wisp of smoke. She felt like she recognised the figure, somehow, but couldn't place it.

Finally, the waterfall began to give way, stretching forward and creating a shadow over the terrified children. They ran for their lives, sprinting further away as the shadow chased them. The ice began to fall apart in the air, causing hail-like chunks to fall and causing miniature craters in the snow.

Then, the ice collided with the ground. The impact shook the ground, an earthquake that buckled the children's knees and sent them sprawling. Roxie was the first to get up, rushing back to help Ellie. Rodgerico rose quickly and sprinted towards his two sisters, grabbing each of their hands and running toward the brow of the hill.

Ewan, lying at the bottom of the hill, screamed as his siblings reached the edge and flung themselves off, rolling down as he had done only minutes before. When they were halfway down the hill, the cascade of ice exploded over the edge, causing sharp splinters and large boulders to rain down upon the children. The sharp corners cut their faces and ripped their clothes.

Roxie threw her head between her legs, groping with her hands to reach her brothers and sister. She risked a glance up and spotted Rodgerico, arms above his head and Ewan nestled below him. She shuffled herself towards them and hunched over near her brothers, her teeth chattering like they were bought from a joke shop.

All of a sudden, the nightmare stopped. The ground laid still and the ice stayed nestled like chips in a cookie. The three arose and breathed a sigh of relief. Rodgerico wiped the blood of a fresh cut that drew across his right cheek. The warm blood dripped onto the snow, spreading over the surface, dying it crimson. Roxie checked Ewan for injuries, ignoring a bruise on her temple that made her head throb with pain.

"Ellie? Ellie? Where are you?"

Rodgerico started screaming, louder and louder the more desperate he got. He finally spotted her, a small ball of fabric, shaking in the wind several metres away. He sprinted across the frosty lawn, sliding down by her side. He took his gloves off and touched her face.

Stone cold.

Her eyes were locked shut. Her hands were buried in the thick snow. Ewan knelt down and just looked at her unconscious body.

"What's wrong with her? Wha… What's happened?"

"We need to get her to a… a hospital or something."

Rodgerico slipped his hands under her and lifted her off the ground.

"Right, up the hill."

Roxie led the way, Ewan on her right holding her hand with Rodgerico bringing up the rear. Ellie still lay slumped in his hands. As they reached the top of the hill, they saw where the waterfall used to be. Instead of a large rock wall, the mountain was caved in and revealed a dimmed room. The children climbed over the hill and headed towards the cave. Their mouths were as open as the chasm.

"Do you wanna go in?" was the only thing that Roxie could think to say, still shell-shocked from the eruption.

"I'm not sure about this. Like… what if it collapses in when we're in there or something?" said Rodgerico.

"I don't really want to go in," Ewan whispered, barely able to be heard from the back of the group, shaking like a leaf.

"Honestly, what choice do we have? We have to go in." Ellie stared blankly up at the huge chasm that lay ahead, making all the children jump.

"Ellie, are you okay?"

"Yeah, just about," she replied with a smile.

Rodgerico gently put her onto the ground

The four children shuddered with a deep breath. All held each other's hands and they headed into the cave as a combined family.

Chapter 14

The First Room

Their eyes adjusted to the dark of the room. A small beam of light from the entrance shone through and produced a circle of light on the opposite wall, illuminating a small door on the other side. The children couldn't see the ceiling and the floor was covered in a thin layer of snow.

"Is it just me, or is this really weird?" Roxie said as they all looked around the room, splitting up and examining the chamber.

Suddenly, a large shard of ice cut through the air, and slammed into the ground, in the dead centre of the room. Everyone twisted round with a jump and tentatively approached the icicle. The room was silent as they tiptoed towards it, the only sound being the echoes of their breath and the creaking of the ice. They all looked over it and Ellie crouched down next to it.

'What the hell?' she exclaimed, wiping her finger on the glistening ice, leaving a cold bite on the tip.

She looked up at the ceiling and saw the dangling stalactites quivering above their heads. Suddenly, a shock shook through the ice causing a lightening-shaped crack to appear through the ground and split right through Rodgerico's legs. All four siblings were shivering and an eerie silence filled the cave.

Ewan dived out of the way as the first rain of ice collapsed onto the floor. The shock caused the two doors to collapse so that the cave was plunged into blackness. Multiple sized chunks of ice fell from above, smashing the ice and chipping away at the screaming children. There was no cover or protection from the onslaught, so the siblings backed into the far corners of the room and crouched down into a foetal-like position. The teeth-shattering noise echoed around the cave, tearing through the children's ears and clattering their bones.

The noise slowly quietened as the last couple of icicles fell towards the ground, splintering into thousands of pieces and decorating the wrinkled floor.

One at a time, the children crept out from their hiding spots, looking up at the now empty cavern ceiling. The shards of ice tinkled as they waded their way through the debris. Roxie, as the oldest, tried to maintain some kind of authority.

"Come on guys, it's all over now. Phew, Jesus! That's was…unexpected. Am I right?"

"How come that's happened twice in, like, five minutes?" Ellie exclaimed, a tint of unbelievability in her cracking tone.

"At least we're all okay, righ…"

A single icicle that was shaking at the top of the cave, far back in the pitch-black shadows, decided at that precise moment to break off from the stone and collapse straight through Roxie's arm.

She cried out in pain and felt to her knees, hissing air through her gritted teeth. Her breathing increased and her hand tightly gripped her seeping wound. A trickle of blood escaped through her clenched hand and slowly dripped into the ground.

As the children hurried and fretted over Roxie's cut (using Ellie's scarf as a makeshift bandage), no one noticed the splatter of blood that landed on the floor disappear as it was soaked up and sank through to a complicated system that even I can't begin to explain. The blood entered this system and was rushed off, forward, into a mysterious exit point.

When the bleeding had steadied, Roxie stood, but was shaky on her feet. With Rodgerico's help, she managed to walk forward.

"I just… wanna leave," Roxie gasped, still holding onto her cut, the other hand gripping her brother's shoulder.

"I don't know if you've noticed, but we can't really leave because the door's collapsed," Rodgerico snapped back.

"I know that. I just said I WANTED to leave not that we CAN!" Roxie screamed back.

"Guys… Please, don't fight," Ellie exclaimed. "We know we're stuck. We just have to wait. Mum will come and find us soon."

"Yeah, Mum will come," Ewan pitched in, sitting on the floor cross-legged.

"You idiots believe that? Even if Mum does come, she's not gonna think we're behind the waterfall. And even if she does, how's she going to get through that foot of ice?" said Rodgerico.

"All right, I was just spit-balling."

"What the hell is spit-balling?"

"PLEASE!" Roxie interrupted. "Just calm down."

"All right, all right."

All four of them sat down. They just sat in the blackness and the silence. It was like being in a prison, or a coffin; like a library with a power cut.

Seconds passed. Minutes passed. Hours passed. Whatever it was, it felt like forever for the four children, sitting in a semi-circle, mostly in silence.

Finally, the door to the next room was released, the ice collapsing showing a small chasm.

"We better go then," Rodgerico said, rising.

"You think?" Roxie spat, brushing past them as she approached the door. The three others followed their sister into the next room.

Chapter 15

The Second Room

This room was brighter than the previous. In fact, a lot brighter. Dazzling light from unknown sources shone from the ceiling and the walls were coated in a white crystal, starting as veins but coming down into a thick sheet near the bottom, as tall as six feet.

The children gasped in awe as they entered, gazing at the mesmerising view that lay before them. Ellie ran up to the wall and planted her grazed hands on the dazzling stone, staring deep into the reflective jewel. She saw herself staring back at her and a smile spread out across her bruised face.

"Ellie, move away from that. We don't know what's going on" Roxie stated, still lingering around the doorway with Rodgerico and Ewan.

"All right," Ellie responded, pushing herself off the mirror. However, her reflection didn't do the same. It stayed with its hand resting on the inside of the crystal, the smile still scarred into her face, contrary to Ellie's now face of shock and panic.

The reflection moved its hand into her mouth and pulled out a large, hairy leg that flopped down, swinging down by her waist. It pulled out two more before the legs kicked into action and became sentient. They were scraping on the floor and scratching the inside of the stone. The reflection-Ellie then began to slowly peel her face upwards, revealing more legs and a condensed face with eight eyes and dripping, fat fangs. At once, the reflection of

Ellie became a huge, towering spider jumping and throwing itself at the glass.

Ellie was in a state of despair, backing up but not daring to look away.

Rodgerico ran over to her and grabbed her.

"Ellie, listen, it's not real. It's a trick or something like that."

"It doesn't look like a trick."

"Well, it is. Look."

Rodgerico walked over to a different part of the crystal and stared into it.

"Look, nothi…"

He was cut off because of what was happening in the mirror. His reflection was sitting down in a wheelchair and his legs were wrapped in thick bandages. His arms were also bandaged, resting on the arm rests like logs. His face was hanging off his left shoulder and his eyes were cold and lifeless.

"Oh… my… God…"

"What. What!" Roxie cried, running over and staring next to her brother.

What looked back at her was the most terrifying image she had ever seen. It was Roxie, herself, but she was alone. Not just alone, but *alone* alone. It was her, but shrunk into a ball with tears in her eyes. A dark cloud filled the background and Roxie's reflection became physically smaller and shrivelled like a melting candle. A featureless face rose up from her knees, blank and cold.

Horrified, Roxie backed away, speechless.

"Stay back, Ewan, stay back. Don't come any closer. Literally, you don't want to see this."

It was too late. Ewan had already crept over to the other side of the room to stare into the crystal. A bed that he recognised was distant in the reflection. It slowly began enlarging and then a hand tearing through the mattress stopped it dead in its tracks. The hand was blue, hairy and thick. Its matted hair was greasy and knotted and its fingers ended in knife-sized claws which almost glistened in the artificial light.

That was enough for Ewan to back away into the arms of his family, his teeth chattering and his eyes bulging. The siblings were all together, in the middle of the room, each glancing round at their respective horror-reflections (horreflections).

Suddenly, one of Ellie's horreflection's legs smashed through the glass, shattering shards everywhere and what followed is indescribable.

The screams from the children and the sounds of cracking distracted all eyes from the sparks flying from the ceiling. The horreflections crackled and teleported around the room, while Rodgerico fell backwards, smashing into the ground on his back. Something large fell from the roof, falling straight through the ice, chucking water into the air. The reflections had disappeared and the light had gone, throwing the children into darkness for the second time in ten minutes.

Rodgerico was the first to be known as being in pain by a scream that scattered around the room, piercing the room's deathly silence. The others crawled across the floor and followed the sounds to reach their brother, feeling around the floor like they were blind men who had lost their sticks. They felt the warm blood, staining their hands and knees while they moved across the cold floor (not noticing the blood seeping into the floor and conjoining with the pipes that fed from the first room). Eventually, the siblings were reunited, clutching each other as tightly as they could.

A solitary light flickered back on, shining a spotlight onto the huddle. It was clear from the angle of Rodgerico's leg that it was broken, and his crying began to worsen.

"Oh my God… Oh my… GOD! It hurts so bad…" screamed Rodgerico, grasping his sisters and tentatively touching his leg.

"Don't worry, we're gonna get you up and then… and then we'll just try and get you out of here, okay?" spluttered Roxie, clearly trying to keep herself together.

Both Roxie and Ellie hooked their brother's arms over their shoulders and holstered him up, while Ewan just stood and watched, still shaken from the encounter with the bed monster. The floor shuddered again and a small door appeared on the opposite side of the room, emitting a tiny stream of light.

"Well, the only way is forward, I guess," Ellie stated, struggling under the weight of her brother.

Together, with Ewan holding Roxie's hand, the foursome headed toward the door dripping in blood, sweat and water.

Chapter 16

The Third Room

An assembly-sized hall met the children, with a tall ceiling and flat, chiselled walls. A slow pulsating sound was heard echoing around the chasm, making the children feel like they were being slightly shaken. An eerie silence filled the cavern, like the gap between lightning and thunder. The group felt suddenly cold, even though no chill wind or icy chill had occurred. A single icicle lay erect in the centre of the room, around 4 feet in length, like a middle finger to the shivering minors.

Before any of them could comprehend how underwhelming the room was, the youngest raced to the middle and stopped directly in front of the stalagmite. His pale hand lifted up and grabbed it half way up, gripping tightly and making his knuckles whiter than his skin. Small cracks erupted from his fist and the shard exploded, throwing icicles over the floor, skating into the corners.

Ewan reached down and picked up a large fragment of sharpened ice, turned to his family and stared them down. His head was slumped down on his left shoulder and drool was slowly falling from his bottom lip. His eyes were empty and cold, white balls in a slowly reddening face.

He slowly smiled and walked forward, his foot slugging on the ground with his arm creaking into a raised position. The sisters, struggling under Rodgerico's wait, stumbled to the left, staggering and tripping over their own feet, Rodgerico freaking out and Ellie collapsing under his weight. The three collapsed on the ground, getting cut up by the random sprays of ice left from the explosion. Ewan started into a sprint and leaped onto Ellie's back, screaming and swiping at her with malice. Ellie stood up and backed herself into the wall, cracking Ewan's back and leaving him in a crumple on the ground. He pushed himself off his back with his hands and landed squarely on his feet, still grinning with blood dribbling with the saliva. Ellie blocked several swipes from her little brother before he swung his free arm at her head, knocking her to the ground. Crying, Ellie shuffled back across the entire room to the other side of the hall, back straight against the wall. As Ewan began running, he crouched onto all fours and began sprinting towards her. Just as he pounced, he was tackled by Roxie and thrown onto the ground, rolling around on the floor. Screaming, Ewan threw his sister off of his chest, slamming her into unconsciousness, leaving a trickle of blood on the floor. Breathless, Ellie stretched up and went to attack the creature which had her brother's face. Almost automatically, he swiped backwards, cutting a deep wound into Ellie's arm. Thick, scarlet blood began to dribble and dripped onto the floor, causing a puddle of pain. Ellie gasped, and fell backwards, landing in a seated position, grabbing onto her arm.

Rodgerico had witnessed it all. After his sisters dropped him, he was powerless on the ground, unable to get up or even move (unless he was going to attack Ewan with a hop). He winced as Ellie backed away and smirked as Ewan was tackled. But after seeing his eldest sister smash into the wall and not move, he began to worry. Using what was left of his strength and confidence, he slowly dragged himself over to the centre of the room, feeling around the debris like a child in a ball-pit. After finding the largest piece he could feel, he pulled himself to his full height, and launched it at the back of Ewan's head. To avoid the blow, Ewan swung to the right, moving with his arms. As he moved, Rodgerico's heart dropped as he saw his sister collapse.

Rodgerico limped forward, hissing breath and taking large lunges to reach his sister. When he reached her, he fell beside her and asked about how she was. By this point, Ewan had got up. He was rubbing his head and had tears in his eyes, ignoring the blood from a wound he had incurred and which slowly slipped away into the ground. Shaking off his 'phase', Ewan walked over to his family.

"GET AWAY... GET AWAY!" Rodgerico screamed, backing off with Ellie in his arms.

"I'm sorry. I... I don't know what happened to me I just... just walked in an... and something took over me so I couldn't move myself. I couldn't do anything. I'm... I'm... so... sorry."

He slumped down beside them and started violently weeping into his arms.

"It's okay, Ewan. I forgive you," Ellie sniffed, smiling behind the pain.

"Something is trying to kill us," Roxie stated, making the others jump as she strolled over from the wall. "And I don't know why. We chose to come in here. We chose to do what we did and, whatever happens, one of us always gets injured. We need to do something about this and I think the only way to go is to go forwards."

The entrance to the chasm was suddenly blocked off by a sliding metal gate erupting from the ground, boxing the four siblings in. As if on cue, a perfect door erupted on the opposite side, revealing a new room.

"Roxie, do we really have to go on?" Ellie questioned.

She looked down at her three defeated siblings, one bleeding, one broken and one scarred.

She took a deep breath and said, "Yes, we do."

Chapter 17

The Final Room

The first thing which all the children laid eyes on was the throne. A translucent, iced seat sitting on a plinth in the middle of an average sized room. The person sitting in the chair had watched them come in, with a smile carved into her face. She smiled at the sight of them, sweating and soaking, out of breath from the numerous adventures they had fought through. The children recognised her instantly, from her pale face and the garnet jumper, which she always wore. The scream from Ewan made it clear to the others who it was, and that they hadn't been mistaken at first glance.

"Mum!"

"Hello children. What a mess you all look."

"Mum, what is this? Was thi… this all you?" Roxie exclaimed, holding back her tears and finding that she was slightly choked up.

Wendy briefly gestured to the room and then to the children themselves.

"Isn't it obvious? Who else would know your greatest fears? Who else would know what you would do in any situation?"

"Mum, please. Why would you do this?"

"Why do you think? You four are the cause of all my misfortunes. Back when I had you two…" she said, pointing at Roxie and Rodgerico "…everything was fine. But that was the cause of it all. When your father came home drunk from one of his stupid nights out and confronted me about the idea of maybe having more kids, something happened. It happened after Rodg. Something changed inside me. Unexplainable, but still existent. So, when he approached me about it, I knew it was going to turn violent. I tried to slowly explain to Sam but he just wouldn't listen. Ignorant as always."

She spat on the ground as she said that, causing a small plink on the cool ground, making Ellie jump due to the silence of the room.

"When he grabbed me, I knew that that was it," she continued, a slight snarl in her voice. "So, I had to do something. I couldn't get free, struggling under my husband's grip. I turned, almost corrupt, and just swung. I only meant to hurt him, or even just knock him unconscious. But when I lost the blade in his chest, I knew that I had taken it too far. And, if it wasn't for you, then that would never have happened!" she screamed, standing up straight on her feet, arching slightly forward.

"But then I went into prison and met Alex, the perfect man, who was actually accepting of what I was. And when we escaped, it all looked good. We took you in again. You loved Alex and Alex fit in like a jigsaw piece. Eventually, everything was smooth sailing. We then decided to have some more kids. Obviously not naturally. We decided to adopt. And, who better, but a baby boy and girl?" With this line, Wendy took a daring glance at the youngest two children, her lip slightly curling as she slowly stepped down from the plinth.

"I got to decide. So, we went through the usual procedure, and came home with Ellie and Ewan. But that wasn't okay for Alex. For some stupid reason, he said that you two were the 'wrong ones' and claimed that I was to blame. After my second husband walked out, I knew that it couldn't be me. Both of my relationships had failed, all because of you four. And, now, it's time to get my revenge, once and for all."

Wendy was metres from them now, fists and teeth clenched.

"You're crazy!" Rodgerico screamed, brushing past his sibling to the front, hobbling on one foot. "What? Are you saying that you set all of this up to... to kill us?"

"This took years to set up. Years of research and preparation. The waterfall was easy to collapse. All I needed was a mallet and strength. The icicle fall was just planned explosives. That and all the doors. The reflections were just holograms and projections from above. And a simple hypnosis machine was needed for the weakest of you to submit to it. You're to blame. All of you." Her hands stretched out into a wide line. "And it's Wendy's time!"

With this line, she launched forward, hands outstretched, a murderous glint in her eye. Rodgerico put his hands out. He had no plan of how to use them and they were quickly whipped aside by Wendy, sending him flying to the left. Quickly, she clasped her thin fingers around Ewan's neck, lifting him a couple of feet into the air. Ewan struggled, his face going redder and redder as Wendy tightened her grip. Roxie, violently, out of nowhere, struck out with a kick, making little impact against her mother's side. Cocking her leg back, Wendy struck back, flinging Roxie away to fall in a crumple, along with her brother.

Ewan was purple now, slowly becoming as weaker as he slumped down. Wendy widened her smile as she...

Ewan dropped to the floor like a leaf in autumn. He lay there, sucking air in large gulps, making a sound like a hippopotamus who had just broken from the water. Gasping, he looked up and saw his mother, frozen, her arms clamped to her left side, holding back streams of blood, pouring from a deep wound plugged by a few inches of sharp ice. Ellie backed against the wall, frozen in terror, eyes welling up, with the same thought dancing (ice-skating) around in her mind: "I just stabbed mum."

Wendy fell onto her healthy side. Her eyes were locked into a position for eternity, always staring at Ellie, always looking, with fear.

"Oh my God... I just meant to... I... I... I am so..." Ellie's sentence drifted off into an awkward silence. The four surrounded the body, looking down in a mix of shock and terror.

"What do we do now?" Ewan puffed, still catching his breath.

Before Roxie could even open her mouth to respond (and if she could, she would have said something about calming down), a large cracking sound like a whip shook the siblings. They looked up and saw a lightning-shaped scar erupt overhead, causing the earth to shake and the walls to tremble. Keeling over, the children looked at each other, panic and worry in their eyes, and the feeling of dread filling up like acid in their stomachs.

The roof caved in. Pieces of all sizes rained from the sky, collapsing onto the five bodies and scraping against the walls.

Moments before her death, Roxie turned and looked at her mother's body. A trigger fell from her bloody hand and she mouthed two words, two words which were the last words she would ever think of.

"Your fault."

The room fell silent. The rocks filled half of the cave, leaving the other half dusty and raw. Only a few hours later, the people of Chillmont who had heard the eruption, went to investigate. They searched all over but couldn't find any evidence of any collapse, only six frozen waterfalls and a completely solid cliff face. The only thing the locals would find was a torn blanket. The only thing the locals would find was a torn blanket which was eventually ignored.

No one ever discovered the fate of the four children and their story will never be known, not even as a fairy-tale, not even as a legend, not even as a myth.

Epilogue

Letter sent to 7 Cranberry Street on 13th August 2021

Dearest Alex,

If you are reading this, I am dead. I had to use the last choice which I never even dreamed I would have to use. But I have. They are all gone. Like you asked for. You're welcome, by the way.

I bet you don't even remember their names, do you? The ones you left in my care. Roxie Phant, Rodgerico Phant, Ellie Phant and Ewan Phant. I bet you didn't. Why am I even telling you this? They don't exist any more, so it's fine.

Thank-you for your cooperation, Alex. You weren't ever the sharpest tool, but I know, deep down, you always made the best decisions. Always the best decisions. Now, make sure you make the correct one this time.

I know everything about you since you left me. I know you married (congratulations!) and I know about your new child (I'm so happy for you!) and I also know where you live. How else would you be receiving this letter? And where your wife works. And where your child goes to school. So let me tell you something that should be easy enough for you to understand.

Confess to the five homicides and your family will live. Simple.

I have contained five vials, each containing our blood. Do with them as you wish. Whatever makes you look the guiltiest.

Thanks again for this Alex. Honestly, I couldn't have done any of this without you.

Many thanks,
    Wendy Phant

Police statement on homicide of the Phant Family — 1ˢᵗ September 2021

Case No: CA693204

Date: 01/09/2021

Reporting Officer: Herbert Trusslley

Prepared By: Chillmont Police Force

Incident/Issue: Homicide of Phant Family

Description of Accident/Issue: The specifics of this case are unknown. Five bodies are yet to be discovered. The arrested suspect, Alex Smith, confessed to all five homicides and was found with a blood-soaked shirt which tested positive for all five victims. The suspect is a known criminal and knew the victims before the action where he helped adopt two of the children (Ellie and Ewan Phant) with another of the victims (Wendy Phant). Trial is still in session, but it is likely that Smith that will be sentenced to life imprisonment in Chillmont Institution.

Suspect Statement: "I had no choice."